**Picture Book
Collection**

*Endowed by
Private Donor*

Mommy Far, Mommy Near

~ An Adoption Story ~

WRITTEN BY Carol Antoinette Peacock

ILLUSTRATED BY Shawn Costello Brownell

Albert Whitman & Company

Morton Grove, Illinois

For my daughters, Elizabeth Li and Katherine Shan-Lin. — C.A.P.

Thanks to my mom; my son, Drew; Dave; my wonderful friends Eileen, Cheryl, Patricia,
and Mary; and most of all, to God. — S.C.B.

*I want to thank the people who helped my husband, Tom Gagen, my grown stepson, Jonathan, and me as
we made our adoption journey. Thanks to Julie Michaels, who first told us about the infant girls waiting in
China. I am grateful to our adoption agency, Wide Horizons for Children, especially Vicki Peterson,
Anna Johnson, Jodie Gleason, and the China Program Coordinator, Linda Lin, who cheered us along the way.*

*I also want to thank the friends we made in China. Thank you to Li Guang Hui, Director of the Wuhan
Foundling Hospital. Director Li placed in our arms first Elizabeth and later, Katherine. I will always
remember Minhua, our devoted nurse, and her son, Shuhai, as well as our lively interpreter and guide,
"Sunshine" Cao Shan.*

*Finally, I am forever grateful to my daughters' birthmothers, who brought Elizabeth and Katherine into
the world. These women gave us the most precious gift of all. They are in my heart every day. — C.A.P.*

Library of Congress Cataloging-in-Publication Data
Peacock, Carol Antoinette.
Mommy far, Mommy near : an adoption story / by Carol Antoinette Peacock ;
illustrated by Shawn Costello Brownell.   p. cm.
Summary: Elizabeth, who was born in China, describes the family who has adopted
her and tries to sort out her feelings for her unknown mother.
ISBN 0-8075-5234-8
[1. Adoption—Fiction. 2. Mother and child—Fiction. 3. Chinese Americans—Fiction.]
I. Brownell, Shawn Costello, ill. II. Title. PZ7.P3117 Mo 2000 [Fic]—dc21 99-036108
CIP

The design is by Scott Piehl.

I AM ELIZABETH, WHICH STARTS WITH AN E. I have black eyes and shiny black hair. I love to do cartwheels and climb trees. I can make popcorn in the microwave, and I like to pick the biggest chocolate chips out of cookie dough. I tell knock-knock jokes, very hilarious. Also, I can do the hokey-pokey.

Now about my family. I have a mommy and a daddy and a little sister named Katherine. Katherine and I were born in China. That's a big country far away.

I don't remember about being born. Mommy made a photo book about how I was adopted from China when I was a baby. The book has lots of pages and a silver cover, and it is very heavy.

"Read," I say to my mother, holding the book in my lap.

Mommy snuggles me, and we read the story together. First there is a picture of my crib, with nothing in it.

"No baby," I say. "You were sad."

Mommy nods. "Mommy and Daddy wanted a baby so much. But we couldn't have one."

I pat Mommy's leg to comfort her.

Next come Mommy and Daddy holding me. "Now we have a baby," my mother says. "Our wonderful baby, Elizabeth."

"Now you are happy," I tell her.

Mommy squeezes me tight.

I am happy, too.

Also in my family is Penny, our dog. I like to roll on the floor with her. Penny's yellow fur is so soft, she makes a big dog pillow.

One day Mommy said, "Do you know how we got Penny? We adopted her. Penny had no family. So we went to a shelter, and we chose her. We made Penny part of *our* family."

"Where is Penny's mommy?" I asked.

Mommy said that she didn't know. The mother dog couldn't take care of Penny, she said.

I grabbed Penny's neck and kissed her on her wet black nose because once Penny had no dog family, and now she had our family to give her hugs and love.

I made up a game for Mommy and me to play every night at bedtime. The game was called "Look."

"Look" meant I lay on my mommy's tummy. Our faces touched. I waited until I could hear my mother's heart thumping softly, like a drum.

"Look," I said. "No songs, no kisses. Just look."

Mommy and I would look and look and look at each other.

One night during Look, Mommy said, "Are our eyes different or the same?"

Different, I told her. Mommy's were two circles, the outside one green, the inside one black. Mine were one large circle, very black.

"Yes, and your eyes are almond and mine are oval," Mommy said. She sat up and drew me closer.

"But our smiles are the same, Mommy. Exactly the same! We both smile with dents in our cheeks. Now, no words, Mommy. Just look."

"When did your mommy get *you* from China?" I asked my mother one day.

Mommy said that she did not come from China. She was born in America.

"I thought all babies came from my China."

"No, honey." My mommy's voice was soft. "Babies come from inside their mommy, Elizabeth."

"But Mommy," I said, "I always thought I came from my China."

I felt afraid.

Mommy lifted me onto her lap. She said I was right, I did come from China. That was the country where I was born.

Mommy talked very slowly. Did I remember the empty crib? she asked. She had not been able to have a baby because she was too old.

Then she said that I had two mommies. I had a mother in China who grew me in her tummy. And I had her, the mother who adopted me.

"Are you telling the truth, Mommy?" I asked.

She nodded.

Two mommies! I had two mommies! I felt dizzy, like when I do too many somersaults. I went outside to climb my favorite tree. *Two mommies, two mommies,* I kept saying over and over and over as I climbed.

I tried to tell Katherine what our mommy had said. Katherine was busy ripping up an old magazine. She was almost three, and she didn't listen that well.

"Katherine," I told her, "Mommy said I have a mommy in China that grew me in her tummy. And you have a mother in China, too. The one who got you born."

Katherine kept ripping.

"And we also have our other mommy right here. The one we call Mommy. We each have *two* mommies, Katherine. One is far away, and one is in our house.

"A far mommy and a near mommy," I said.

Katherine and I talked on our toy telephones a lot. Once in a while I pretended it was my mommy from China calling.

"Katherine," I would say, "it's my mommy from China."

Katherine would yell, "Hello, Elizabeth's China mommy! What are you doing?"

I would tell the China mommy about blowing bubbles with Katherine or about how Daddy and I take rain walks and how I string necklaces out of shiny beads.

One day when the toy phone went rr-ing, my mommy from China wanted to talk to our mommy here!

Mommy held the phone. "Oh, hello, Elizabeth's China mommy. Yes, Elizabeth is doing fine. She loves you very much. And she knows you love her, too."

"If my other mother loved me so much, why couldn't she keep me?" I asked my mother one night.

Mommy said that China had many people—millions and trillions of people. Too many people for one country. So the China people made up a rule. Each family could only have one child.

"But China is a very big country!" I said. "They should have room for all the babies."

My mother touched my cheek. "I know. But that was the rule, honey. One family, one child. Your mother couldn't keep you because she already had a baby."

"Another baby before *me?*"

Mommy nodded. "The rule was strict, and she couldn't break it. Your mother wanted to keep you very much."

"What did she do with me, Mommy?"

"She did the best thing she could—she bundled you up snugly and left you where she knew someone could find you and take care of you."

"Did she kiss me . . . and hug me, Mommy?"

"She did, honey."

I asked what my mother's name was.

Mommy put her arms around me and said nobody knew her name or where she was. Would I like to make up a name for her, the other mommy?

"No," I said.

She was too far away to have a name. Far like the moon, or the first star for wishing.

Then I made up a different game. It was called "Adopt Me."

I would ask my mommy about how she and Daddy adopted me.

"We wanted a baby so badly," said Mommy. "We heard that in China there were babies who needed homes. They were being cared for in places called orphanages. So we wrote a letter. Then Daddy and I waited and waited. Finally one day the people from China wrote us back. They told us they had a baby that needed a mommy and daddy."

"The picture," I reminded her.

Mommy smiled. "They gave us a picture of you, so little. So we got on a plane and we flew all the way to China. A woman at the orphanage placed you in our arms—"

"And you were so happy—"

"I was so happy, I cried and cried. Daddy and I held you very tight."

Then I would say, "Show me how you adopted me. Adopt me, Mommy."

So my mommy would hug me and say,

You are my child.

You are my own.

I love you forever.

I adopt you now.

"Again," I would say. "Adopt me again."

And my mother would adopt me again and again.

I started to adopt my own babies. On Monday, I adopted Snowbear. I hugged him and said,

You are my child.
You are my own.
I love you forever.
I adopt you now.

On Tuesday, I adopted Chinese Rag Doll. On Wednesday, I adopted Happy Duck. On Thursday, I adopted Sad Duck. On Friday, I adopted Dalmatian Dog. On Saturday, I adopted Kitty. On Sunday, I adopted Fishy in the Sea.

Then I put them all on my rocker beside me. I cuddled them up and sang them a sweet lullaby. They were my babies, my family, all.

In the summer something happened.

I was at the playground with Mommy. I climbed the tallest slide, and I was high in the sky. Then, across the field, I saw a mommy and a little girl. They had black eyes and shiny black hair, like me. The mother was holding the little girl's hand.

She must be a Chinese mother.

My other mommy would look just like her.

I stayed still like a statue and watched. The mother and her little girl came closer.

I took my hand off the railing, and I gave a nice little wave.

The mommy didn't see me. Her head was bent down, and she didn't even notice me.

"Are you okay, honey?" my mother called.

I sat, staring.

"Come on down, Elizabeth," said Mommy.

I put my sneakers on the steps of the ladder. Slowly I climbed towards the ground. My mother was there to catch me.

"You saw the Chinese mother and her daughter, didn't you?" Mommy said softly.

Together we watched till the mommy and the little girl were gone. Then my mother lifted me up and carried me all the way home.

"Hold me like when I was a baby," I told her when we were back home.

So we sat on her bed, and Mommy rocked me like a tiny baby, back and forth, back and forth.

"You saw the Chinese mommy and she reminded you of your other mommy and now you are sad, I think," said Mommy.

I closed my eyes. "My mommy is lost," I said.

"That mommy loved you very much," my mother said.

"She didn't keep me."

"No, but she wanted to. Very badly." Mommy wiped my tears with her hand.

My mother said, "That mommy loved you, Elizabeth. And I love you. And Daddy loves you. And Katherine loves you. And Penny loves you." She said it slowly, like she was singing a song.

I opened my eyes. "Adopt me," I said.
Mommy wrapped her arms around me and said,
You are my child.
You are my own.
I love you forever.
I adopt you now.

Now, sometimes at bedtime, I tell Mommy, "I want to lie on your tummy."

So I lie on my mother's tummy. Our faces touch. I wait until I can hear my mommy's heart beating. I say, "Look."

We look. No songs, no kisses. Just look.

In a deep voice, I say, "My mother."

Just as deep, my mommy says, "My daughter."

And then we hug, as tight as can be, me and my mother, who is very near.